Tea
with the Queen

Written by
Chrissi Hart

Illustrated by
Stephen Macquignon

To Judy, my friend and mentor with love, Chrissi

x*ist Publishing

To Charlie Carter-Bates, who sings with the angels.

For more about Charlie, visit www.charliechargeson.com

First Edition
Paperback ISBN: 978-1-62395-608-0
eISBN: 978-1-62395-609-7
ePib ISBN: 978-1-62395-610-3
Published in the United States
by Xist Publishing
www.xistpublishing.com

"Hang onto your hat, Charlie," grandfather said. "We're in for a bumpy ride."

"Too late," Charlie said, trying to catch his yellow school cap that spun into the clouds.

Charlie and his grandparents, Harriet and Arthur, stared straight ahead, as they traveled on the Royal Air Express.

This was no ordinary vehicle.

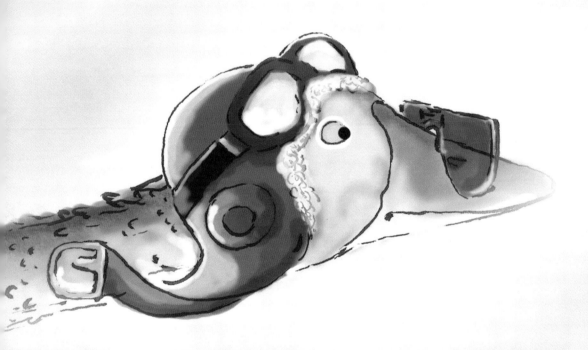

It was a large goose named Percy.

This was the first time Charlie and his grandparents had flown by goose, and it was strange, yet comfortable.

"Never mind your hat, dear," Harriet said, "just hold on tight. Where are we going again?"

"Grandma, don't you remember? We're going to Buckingham Palace to have tea with the Queen."

"Oh yes, fancy that! But why?"

"Because you are 100 years old!" Charlie said.

"That's what happens when you reach 100. You get to have tea with the Queen, and you can bring two guests!"

Suddenly, a gust of wind blew them sideways.

"Won't your glasses fly off?" Charlie asked Percy.

"Don't worry, Master. I have taken this trip many times at this altitude and my glasses haven't flown off yet. Hold on, I'll show you!"

Percy did a 360-degree loop, causing Charlie to squeal
with delight.

Harriet and Arthur went white as a sheet.

"Oi!" Arthur shouted, "Don't do that again."

Grandma had packed their bags a week ago when she received a
letter from the Queen inviting her for tea. She was glad they had
dressed warmly in tweed coats and hats. It was cold in the clouds.
Charlie could smell the salt in the air as they traveled along the
East Anglican coast to London.

Seagulls flew all around them making loud shrieking cries that hurt his ears. He was nervous--- the gulls came close to take a look at the strange spectacle of three mice traveling on the back of a goose. "What if the seagulls get hungry?" Charlie asked, realizing he could be next on their lunch menu.

He was sure he heard one say, "He'd be alright with a few chips!" He wasn't too happy about flying on a big bird either.

He preferred to be on the ground, tucking into a ripe hunk of stilton cheese.

"We're going to fall off!" Charlie yelled.

"Look at the great view down there," Grandma Harriet said, trying her best to distract Charlie.

Thatched roofs, stone cottages and wooden windmills were below.

The brown murky water of the English Channel slapped
against the cliff edge. They flew over farms and villages along
the rugged coastline.

As they entered London, green parks lay below, and cherry
red mailboxes and telephone kiosks dotted the streets.

After a while, Percy announced, "Ladies and gentlemen, we are approaching Big Ben and the Houses of Parliament."

"Who is Big Ben?" Charlie asked.

"Not who, what!" Arthur corrected.

Percy warned, "Brace yourselves for a crash landing!"

"What!" Charlie exclaimed.

His worst fear was about to come true. The goose
swooped down onto the Buckingham Palace pond.
Water sprayed everywhere.

"Stop!" Harriet shrieked as they tumbled into the Queen's rose garden.

"Ouch! You need to work on that landing." Charlie said, wiping the sweat from his brow.

Then, from nowhere, two large, snarling dogs, with saliva dripping from their jagged teeth appeared.

"The Queen's corgis," Percy announced. "Sorry, got to go."

"Follow the signs for the Royal pantry and kitchens.

A footman will escort you to your rooms," Percy said.

Harriet promptly fainted and fell into Arthur's arms just
before she hit the ground. Charlie had to think fast.
Reaching into his pocket he felt two sticks of black
liquorice left over from his bag of sweets.
He threw them as far as he could.
The dogs raced after them, their large ears flapping in the breeze.
"That will keep you busy for awhile!"
Charlie yelled, shaking his fist at them.

Charlie and his grandparents raced to the downstairs pantry where a grand reception was waiting for them.

They were just in time to have tea—
with the mouse Queen!